My First Kitten

ROSMARIE HAUSHERR

FOUR WINDS PRESS
Macmillan Publishing Company/New York
Collier Macmillan Publishers/London

Photographing this story was possible only because Adam Guest, his family, and his Tiger participated with enthusiasm and patience. My thanks to all of them for turning this book project into a rewarding experience.

A special thank you to Raymond Marunas, who helped with the writing, and to Dr. John Stetson and his staff for sharing their professional experiences and time.

My thanks to Mr. Kittredge, the Bowles family, Ethan Marunas, the Magnus family, William J. Lederer, the Willard family, the Schlosser family, Dilys Evans and the many friends who helped.

And thank you, Catherine Stock, for a charming book design.

Macmillan Publishing Company
866 Third Avenue, New York, N.Y. 10022
Collier Macmillan Canada, Inc.
Printed in the United States of America
10 9 8 7 6 5 4 3

The text of this book is set in 14 pt. Century Schoolbook.
The illustrations are black-and-white photographs reproduced in halftone.

Library of Congress Cataloging in Publication Data
Hausherr, Rosmarie.
My first kitten.
Summary: Seven-year-old Adam has a summer full of new experiences and responsibilities when he receives a kitten for a pet.
1. Kittens–Juvenile literature. 2. Cats–Juvenile literature. [1. Cats. 2. Pets] I. Title.
SF445.7.H38 1985 636.8'07 85-42804
ISBN 0-02-743420-6

My name is Adam. I am seven years old. I live with my mother and father and Jill, my younger sister, in a small house in the hills of northern Vermont. From my bedroom window I can see fields, apple trees and our muddy pond. I like my home.

We have a dog, ducks and two goslings, which is what baby geese are called. Our dog's name is Mike. He is friendly and old and sleeps a lot. Mike is really my father's dog. The fluffy yellow goslings are Jill's. They nibble at her long hair when she holds them.

I ride my mountain bike up and down the dirt road or play with Jill. I wish I had my own pet.

Today, riding home on the school bus, my friend Tommy told me that Mr. Kittredge, one of our neighbors, has kittens for adoption.

I found my mom in her sewing room, working on a quilt. I asked her, "Mom, may I have a kitten?"

Mom kept sewing. "A kitten is not a toy, Adam. It won't go away when you are tired of it. It has to be cared for and, like Mike, would live with us for many years. A pet also costs money."

"I promise I would take good care of my kitten. Please, Mom, please, let me have one," I begged.

Mom thought a moment and then said she'd discuss it with Dad.

My parents have decided I am old enough to take care of a pet. I think they're the best parents in the whole world!

I want to go to Mr. Kittredge's farm right now, but Mom says we can't until Saturday. We have to get ready for the kitten. Dad is buying a litter pan, kitty litter and cat food. Jill is going with him. Mom is making an appointment with Dr. Stetson, our veterinarian—that's what an animal doctor is called. And my jobs are finding books about cats in the library and making the kitten a bed.

I think Jill is jealous. She is telling everyone she is going to get a pony.

Finally it's Saturday. In the morning we drive down the road to Mr. Kittredge's farm. Mr. Kittredge takes us to the big red barn, where he keeps his cats. The barn smells of animals and hay. The cats help keep it free of mice.

"The kittens are eight weeks old. They are healthy and already weaned," Mr. Kittredge says.

"What is *weaned*?" Jill wants to know.

"The kittens don't drink milk from their mother any-more. They eat solid food. Here they are."

Four kittens are playing in the hay. Their mother is out hunting. The kittens have large eyes, tiny pointed ears and pink noses. Three of them are black and white, and the fourth one has beautiful orange stripes.

"That's the one I want, the little tiger, and that's what I'll call it."

My orange kitten purrs and tickles my ear with its whiskers.

"Adam, you sure picked a handsome little fellow. Take good care of him," Mr. Kittredge tells me.

"Is it a he?" I ask.

"Yep, sure is."

We say thank you to Mr. Kittredge and good-bye to the other kittens.

At home, my father shows me how to hold a kitten properly. He places one hand under Tiger's tail and the other under his front legs. Kittens don't like to be squeezed, held by the tail or handled roughly. "Think how you would like to be treated," Dad says.

When I show Tiger the living room, the kitchen and the back hall, where we placed his litter pan, he looks around shyly. I take him to his bed. Maybe he is tired. But was I wrong!

Mom says that kittens have a lot of energy, but they have small hearts and lungs. They get exhausted and have to take many naps.

Tiger is hungry. I feed him a small portion of cat food and watch as he licks the moist meat, pulls small chunks to the edge of the plate and eats them slowly. Mom says I'll have to feed him several times a day because he is growing fast.

Kittens are always hungry, but they do not overeat the way I sometimes do.

When Tiger drinks, he curls his rough, little tongue and flips liquid into his mouth with great speed. He needs a lot of water. I'll have to refill his bowl often.

Tiger is very neat. He washes after eating and purrs happily.

Dad says it's bedtime, and I have to say good night to Tiger. He will sleep in the living room, where it's warm.

"Don't worry if he cries at night," Dad says. "He'll be all right."

Upstairs in bed I can't fall asleep. I wonder if Tiger is lonely, all by himself. The house seems so quiet.

Meow, meow, meow. It's Tiger, crying.

Quickly, I go downstairs. Tiger looks lost. I know he is missing his mommy. I pick him up carefully and take him upstairs with me.

The next morning, Tiger has piddled on my rug.

"Show him the litter box," Mom tells me. "Tiger doesn't know his way around the house yet. I'll show you how to sponge up the mess with water and vinegar."

The litter box is a flat tray filled with fine, scented pebbles. Tiger digs a hole, goes to the bathroom, and covers it up afterward. He knows what to do all by himself. When he is older, he can go outdoors.

Tiger's appointment with the veterinarian is the next day. Dr. Stetson will examine Tiger to make sure he doesn't have parasites.

"What are *parasites?"* Jill wants to know.

Mom has to think for a minute. "Well, parasites are little animals, like worms or bugs," she says. "They live inside other animals, or on them, and sometimes they spread to people, too."

"Tiger doesn't have parasites," I say quickly.

"Probably not," Mom answers. "But we want to make sure. That's why we have to bring a sample of Tiger's bowel movement, or *stool,* to Dr. Stetson."

People with their pets are sitting in Dr. Stetson's waiting room. While Mom talks to the receptionist, Tiger happily plays with his tail.

I like Dr. Stetson. He handles my kitten gently as he looks into Tiger's mouth, eyes and ears. Then he lifts Tiger's tail and feels his stomach.

Dr. Stetson writes everything down on a piece of paper. Mom says the paper is called a chart. Both my name and Tiger's appear at the top.

"Dr. Stetson, how can you tell if Tiger has parasites?"

"By looking at his coat, Adam. And by examining that stool sample under my microscope for worms."

Dr. Stetson prepares to give Tiger a shot with a long needle. "Don't worry, Adam, it won't hurt him. It will keep him healthy. See—all done."

Dr. Stetson tells me that Tiger is fine and asks me to bring him back in two weeks for another shot.

Tiger explores the house silently on his soft paws. It's a big place for such a little cat. If I don't see or hear him for a while, I call "Tiger!" and often he comes back to me and purrs. I think Tiger knows he is my cat, but he also plays with Jill.

I am proud of Tiger and like to show him to my friends and neighbors. When Great-Grandpa stops by, he tells me he, too, had a kitten when he was a little boy. I can't imagine Great-Grandpa as a little boy, but I don't say so.

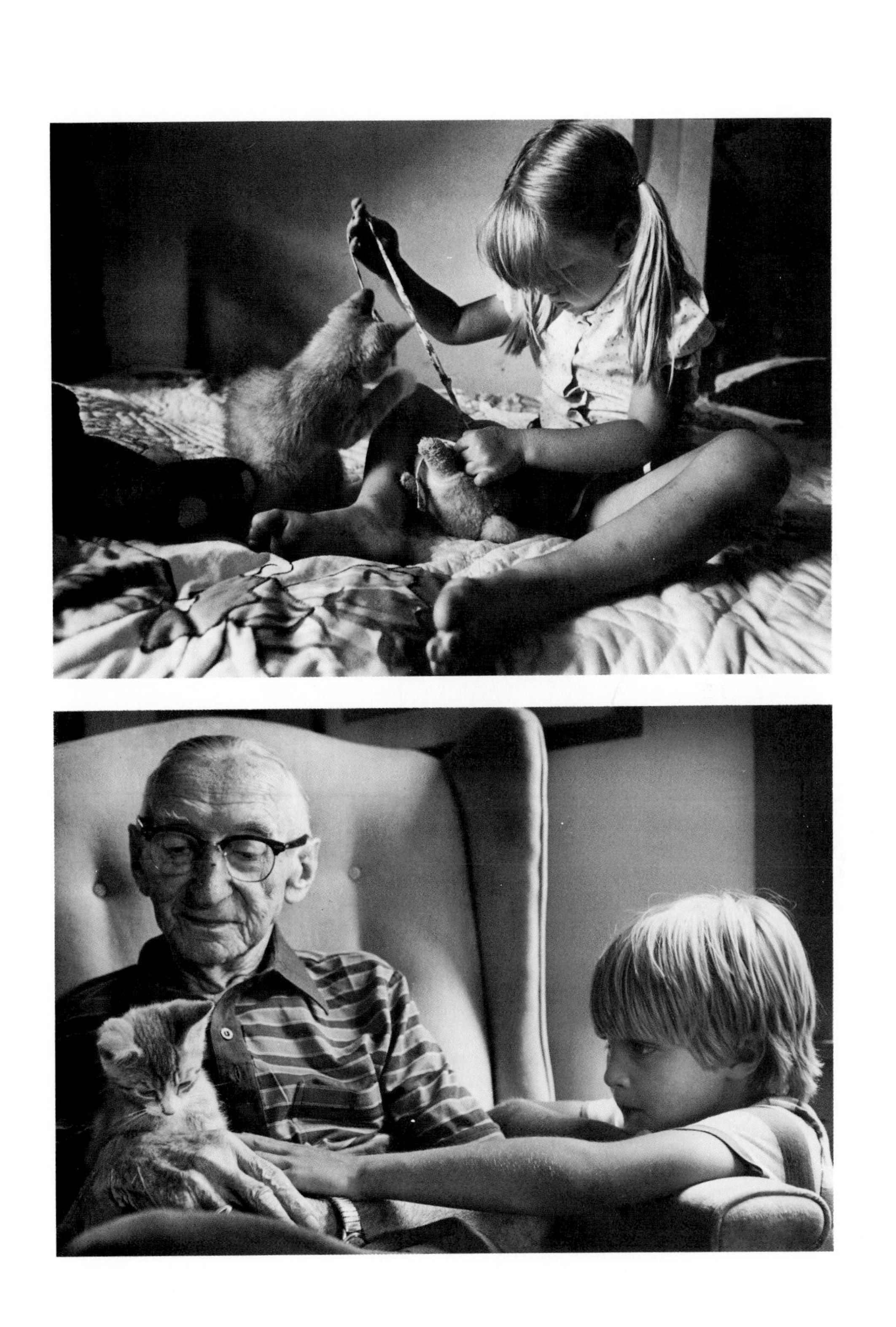

Mike has been staying outside in his doghouse, but Dad thinks it's time he met Tiger. When he brings Mike indoors, Dad watches him. Introducing a new pet has to be done carefully: A kitten can be hurt by a jealous older pet. Most of the time, though, older animals will accept a kitten or a puppy.

Tiger loves to play. He plays with everything that moves. He goes wild sometimes and drives me crazy. I love Tiger, but it isn't always easy to be patient. "Stop that, Tiger! That's enough. Go play with Jill."

PURINA
CHOWS

Soon I hear a scream from Jill's room. "Adam, come and get your cat! He's jumping all over my cards!"

Tiger would probably like to play outside. But we're keeping him in the house for the first two weeks. Kittens who are used to people make better pets, Mom says. Besides, he is too little to be safe outside on his own.

But baby animals can get hurt in the house. We all must be careful not to sit or step on Tiger or lock him in a closet or let him chew electric cords.

Tiger is curious and very playful. Even Mom's or Grandpa's work is play for him. He still has to learn the rules: no jumping onto kitchen counters, no running on top of furniture, no nibbling on house plants.

"Say NO and put him on the floor," Mom says.

Finally, Tiger is allowed outside. Right away he starts exploring the garden. I wonder what the garden looks like from so close to the ground.

Outside there are safety rules, too. Before starting the car, Mom and Dad walk around it to make sure no animals are sleeping underneath. Many cats are hurt or killed by cars. I try to keep Tiger off the road.

I like to climb trees, and so does Tiger. He is lighter and quicker than I am and can go onto small branches.

One day Tiger gets stuck high in a tree. He needs help. I run for my dad. He always knows what to do.

Cats have wonderful balance, and they can walk along high, narrow spaces. When they fall they usually land on their feet—but not always. Sometimes they get hurt.

Tiger is growing bigger. He is not a baby anymore. He is taller and slimmer, has pretty light brown eyes, long whiskers and white feet. He also seems to have grown smarter.

Jill's goslings have also grown. They've turned into large geese. Jill says she still likes them, but she doesn't get too close.

Tiger goes out with me every day now. When I run barefoot outside, I have to scrub my dirty feet before I go to bed. Tiger's paws always look white. He licks and cleans himself all the time. His long, pink tongue reaches deep into his fur. The only place his tongue can't reach is the back of his head and neck. To clean there, he licks his paw and uses it like a washcloth. Tiger is a smart cat.

Sometimes, though, he needs our help. Mom shows me how to groom Tiger, moving the brush from his head to his tail, as the hair lies. Grooming removes loose hair and it makes Tiger's fur shiny. It's a good way to check for fleas and ticks.

Tiger loves to be groomed. He purrs and purrs.

After grooming Tiger, Mom carefully cleans his ears and checks them for ticks, mites and other parasites. I can tell Tiger doesn't like it. He stops purring.

Sometimes I think that Tiger is my best buddy.

I'm not feeling well today. My stomach is upset, and I have to stay at home. I call Leslie to tell her I can't play at her house. Today I'm glad Tiger is with me. I hear his heartbeat and feel his weight on my chest.

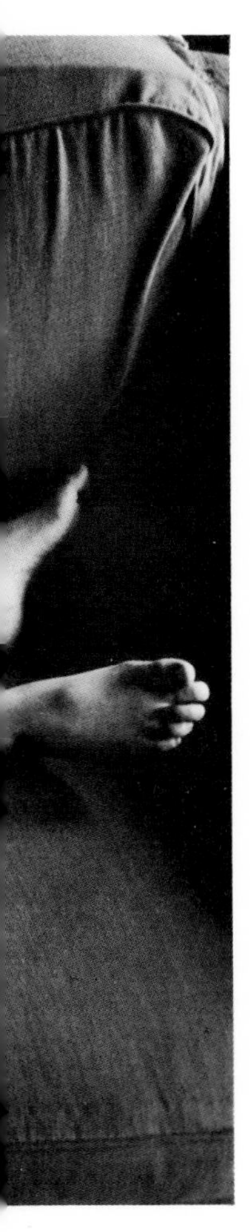

I like to look into his eyes. In bright light his pupils are just like tiny slits. In the dark they open very wide – that's why he can see at night. Cats are *nocturnal* animals. Tiger's playing and chasing at night sometimes wakes me up.

I can tell what Tiger wants from the way he meows. I know when he is hungry, when he wants to play, when he is bored or when he wants to go outside.

Tiger is turning into a hunter. One day he catches a mouse. I am curious, but Tiger doesn't want to share his mouse with anyone. He picks it up and disappears behind the shed. Mom says that cats play with mice before they eat them. Tiger will hunt birds, chipmunks, moles and other small animals. But that doesn't make him a bad cat, just a normal one.

Some weeks later, it's time to take Tiger to Dr. Stetson for an operation called *neutering*. Tiger is a healthy male cat and is old enough now to mate with female cats to make kittens. That means he'll start to wander off to nearby farms and leave a strong-smelling scent to mark his territory. He could also get into fights with other male cats. The operation will prevent this and make Tiger a calmer, happier cat.

Dr. Stetson has told us not to feed Tiger the night before the operation. He can't have breakfast either. If there is food or water in Tiger's stomach when Dr. Stetson puts him to sleep for the operation, he might get sick.

Tiger cries in the car. He can't understand why he is hungry and why he is trapped. I feel bad and keep talking to him.

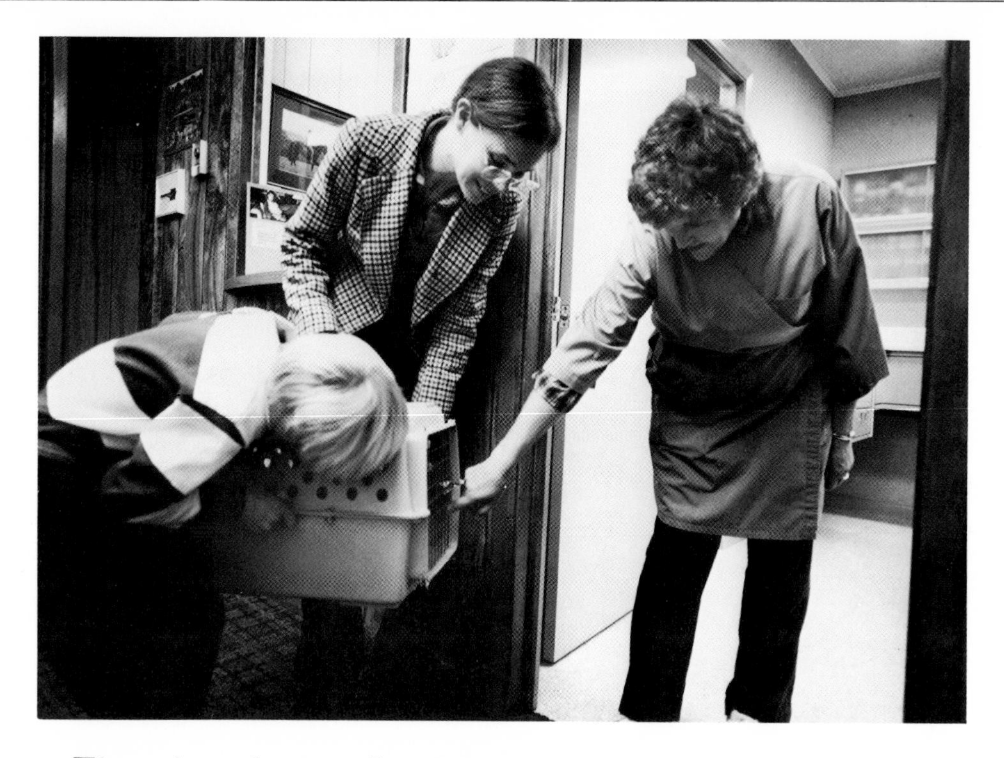

Tiger is so heavy that Mom has to help me carry him.

"Well, look who is back," says Bernice, Dr. Stetson's assistant. "I like your new cage. That's a safe way to travel."

"Will the operation hurt my cat, Dr. Stetson?"

"The operation won't, Adam, but he will be uncomfortable for a few days after it. I'll put a mask over his nose to anesthetize him. That puts him to sleep so he doesn't feel any pain. The operation is only a small cut. If you had a female cat, it would be more complicated. You can take Tiger home by the end of the day."

Dr. Stetson shows me the operating room. It has a special table that moves up and down and in any direction. There are strong lights so Dr. Stetson can see what he is doing. The medical instruments are laid out in a row. Everything is very clean. It makes me feel better about Tiger's operation.

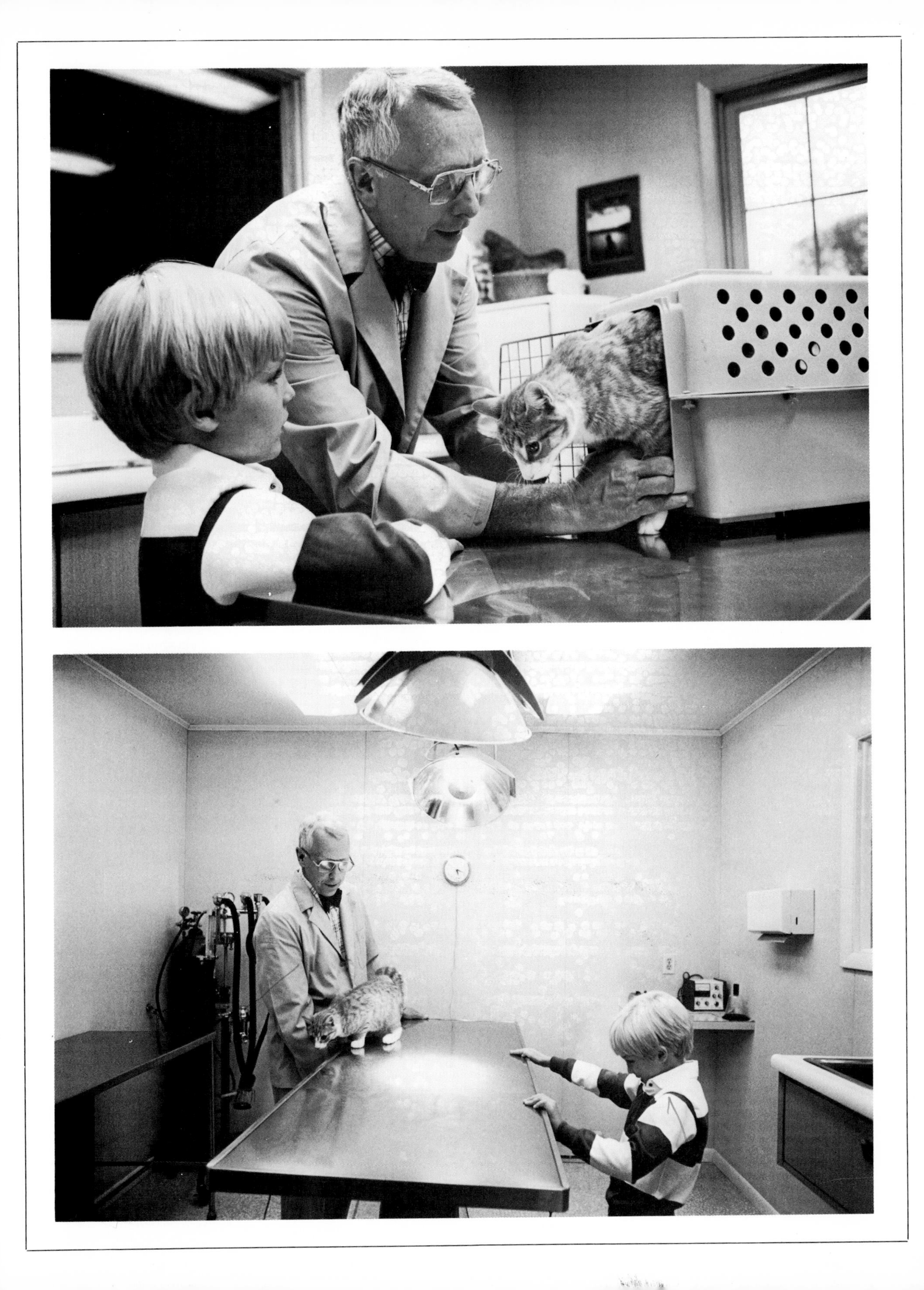

We pick Tiger up while Grandma is cooking dinner at home. I am so happy to have him back.

He seems a bit confused and sits quietly in his bed. He purrs when I cuddle him. Mom says he will be his old self in a few days.

Before bedtime Grandma reads a story for Tiger, Jill and me. It's been a rough day. The teacher yelled at me for not paying attention in class. I was only thinking about Tiger.

Tiger is well again. He is calmer. When I go to school in the morning he says good-bye. Then, Mom says, he goes up to my room for a snooze with my stuffed animals.

The days are getting colder. Tiger stays inside more. He likes to sit next to me when I do my homework. He knows I'll play with him when I'm finished.

Tiger knows that I love him. When I go away, he knows I'll always come back to take care of him. We will be friends for ever and ever.

THE BERENSTAIN BEARS

What Parents Should Know

in consultation with Dr. John Stetson, veterinarian

Adopting a pet means caring for an animal as long as it lives. With the parents' guidance and loving help, growing up with a kitten can be a happy experience for any child.

Consider before Adopting a Kitten

- Is your child mature enough for a pet? (Seven is about the right age.)
- Can you afford veterinarian fees, cat food and other expenses?
- Do you have enough space for a new pet?
- Is your family schedule such that your kitten will have company during part of the day?

Where to Get a Kitten

- Adoption centers check their animals' physical and mental health before putting them up for adoption.
- Breeders handle pedigree cats. Learn the characteristics of the different breeds before choosing one.
- Newspaper ads, neighbors and friends are good sources because you will know something about the mother cat and her litter. In pet stores, you can learn little about an animal's history.

How to Pick the Right Kitten from a Litter

Select a weaned kitten (about eight weeks old) that is healthy and alert, with bright eyes and a shiny coat.

When You Bring Your Kitten Home

A pet is *not* a toy! Teach your child to treat the baby animal with love and respect.

- Health: Immediately take your kitten to a veterinarian for a check-up and necessary shots. Make sure your child comes along.
- Other pets: Introduce the kitten to your pets after its check-up.
- Food: Feed the kitten according to your veterinarian's guidelines.
- Grooming: Start early; combs and brushes are sold in pet stores. Be sure your cat has a scratching post for sharpening its nails.
- Litter box: Provide a box large enough, accessible at all times, and keep it clean. If your cat goes outdoors, cover up your child's sandbox.
- Accidents: Small animals can get hurt easily.
  Dangers in the home: Unattended electrical and gas appliances, electrical cords, improperly stored household chemicals, small chewable items that can be swallowed, plastic bags, mousetraps, and poisonous plants. Always check large appliances, such as washing machines, before turning them on. Don't use fumigants containing cyanide. Secure open windows with sturdy screens.
  Dangers outside the home: Keep your kitten indoors at night. Cover deep holes in the garden. Check before starting cars or other machines. Store chemicals and herbicides safely. Let your cat out from a door facing away from the road.
- House rules: With your child, establish house rules for your pet and stick to them.
- Travel: Use a safe pet carrier. Never leave your cat alone in a hot car.
- Neutering: If you do not wish your cat to have kittens, have it spayed (if female) or neutered (if male) by your veterinarian. This will make your cat a calm, affectionate pet.

There are many entertaining and informative books published on kittens and cats. The more you and your child know about your pet, the richer your experience of friendship with the animal will be.